Charles George Mayers

The Songs of Taychobera

Or, Romances of the Four Lakes

Charles George Mayers

The Songs of Taychobera
Or, Romances of the Four Lakes

ISBN/EAN: 9783337021269

Printed in Europe, USA, Canada, Australia, Japan

Cover: Foto ©Andreas Hilbeck / pixelio.de

More available books at **www.hansebooks.com**

THE SONGS OF TAYCHOBERA

OR

ROMANCES OF THE FOUR LAKES

BY

MAJ. CHAS. G. MAYERS

DAVID ATWOOD
PRINTER AND STEREOTYPER
1889

GEN. GEO. P. DELAPLAINE:

My Dear Friend — Is it too late in life to indulge in such frivolity as rhyming about our Lakes? When I sent you Mendota I thought it an unfinished task, and old or young I have found great pleasure in still pursuing it. I now send it to you with its associates. I fear you will find them full of faults, but I am afraid that I could not improve them if I tried. I therefore offer them to you in token of our still continued friendship.

CHAS. G. MAYERS.

Madison, Wis, April 8, 1889.

THESE poems are the offspring of many happy hours spent in communing with Nature upon and around the lakes whose faintly-whispered stories they endeavor to relate. If they are fancy-woven, the warp and woof were furnished by the same nature that painted the ever-varying pictures from which they take their hue.

When the country embracing the four lakes and their connecting stream, the " Yahara," beautifully described by General S. Mills as being "strung like jewels on a cord of silver," was first settled by white men, the Indians gave as the definition of Taychobera, " THE COUNTRY OF THE FOUR LAKES," but of late years when asked the meaning of the word, they reply, " MADISON."

The poems consist of

    1st. KEGONSA,

        THE FISH LAKE.

    2d. WABESA,

        THE LAKE OF THE WHITE SWAN.

    3d. MONONA,

        THE BEAUTIFUL LAKE.

    4th. MENDOTA,

        THE SPIRIT LAKE.

KEGONSA.

’ER the white man knew the country,
  E’er the hoof of horse or cattle
Left in furrow or in woodland
  Track of plow or path of battle;
E’er the axe of hardy woodman —
  Blow to blow in echoes calling —
Through the forest arches rang the
  Death notes of a comrade falling;
E’er the bee with honey laden
  Sang its sunny song of humming,
Telling all who knew the music
  That another race was coming.
First the Trapper, then the Squatter —
  Thus might run the brown bee’s ditty
Then the Woodsman, then the Farmer,
  Then the Mill, and then the City.
For the warrior and the hunter,
  Painted as became his station,
Fought and hunted, all life deeming
  That within his observation.

Knew naught of the world beyond him.
From the Lakes unto the Ocean
Spanned the limits of his legends;
    Knew not of the wild commotion,
Of the ceaseless strife and struggle,
    'Mong the Marts, and Halls of Learning,
Ever reaching onward, upward,
    Yesterday's achievements spurning.

When the sad and dreary Winter
    Drove to covert every creature,
And the cheerless snowy mantle
    Overspread the face of Nature;
All the venison was eaten,
    And the wild rice so diminished
It could last but few days longer,
    And the corn was nearly finished;
When the Hunter, starting hungry,
    Hungry still returned, and weary,
Sad and weary, from the cheerless
    Hunt of woods and naked prairie;
Pinched and famished were the women,
    And the children fever stricken,
For the ruthless Winter vampire
    On their brows his doom had written.

Where the snows were light and fleeting,
  Where the game all winter tarried,
Dwelt a powerful tribe of Red-men,
  Whose domain no stranger harried,
For the fate of all who ventured —
  Youthful Brave or Warrior hoary —
Was the same, not one returning
  To relate adventurous story.
And the tribe, by hunger wasted,
  Though their chief was young, and stronger
Far than any other warrior,
  And could fight the famine longer,
Never turned their faces toward the
  " Land of Hunting," with intention
To oppose so fierce a nation,
  That its name they shunned to mention!
Machikawa was their chieftain,
  Young in summers, but in tracking
Man or beast through tangled forest,
  In resource was never lacking.
Read the bent twig as the written
  Lore is read by men of learning,
Read it plainer, for his reading
  Never needed backward turning.

But the chief, though fierce as panther
  Or as wolf on quarry rushing!
Could not fight the cold and hunger
  That his tribe was slowly crushing!
Though he toiled and hunted for them,
  Long and hard, yet still returning
Baffled, or with game so little
  That his cheek was often burning
With resentment at his fortune!
  On the earth his quarry throwing,
Waited neither thanks nor question,
  Hungry to his wigwam going!
In the tribe was Waba-Ogen,
  Or the White Rose of the Nation;
She was beautiful as ever
  Lit the eye with admiration!
She was beautiful as Summer!
  Lighter than the other daughters
Of the tribe, and young and laughing
  As the bright and sparkling waters!
And the young chief, Machikawa,
  Loved her fondly as e'er lover
Worshiped maiden; she had promised,
  When the dreary months were over,

She would come into his wigwam,
  And the merry songs and dances
Of their bridal should awaken
  Brows of woe to happy glances;
But the sad and freezing Winter
  On her face had plainly written
Want and Suffering; not submission
  To the sores by Winter bitten,
While she hushed the wail of childhood,
  Cheered with hope her sex despairing,
Tongue or eye addressing warriors,
  Ever prompted them to daring!
Urged or challenged them to action,
  If one path was closed unto them.
All the rest were broad and open,
  And the fearless might pursue them.
Sad and dreary came the sunset;
  Sadly watched they his declining.
At the absence of their chieftain
  Some were wondering, some repining.
Well equipped, at early morning
  He had gone, by storm deterred not.
But three Suns had followed westward,
  And his step or voice they heard not.

In the heart of Waba-Ogen
  Fears were crowding fast and faster
Lest her lover, at her bidding,
  Had encountered dire disaster!
With the first faint blush of day-break
  Went the " White Rose " to discover,
And to rescue, if it might be,
  Or to die beside her lover!
From the steep bluff's snowy summit,
  In the faint and misty distance
She perceived a toiling figure,
  Sorely needing stout assistance;
And her heart, by love instructed,
  Knew her noble chief returning,
And the joy the knowledge gave her
  Set her blood with rapture burning.
Flying back among the wigwams,
  Willing men she sent to meet him;
Then she pondered, sorely puzzled,
  How with pride enough to greet him.
Two deer and two wolves were trophies
  That his toilsome hunt rewarded.
All were eaten — quickly eaten,
  E'en the wolf-flesh not discarded.

Waba-Ogen cooked the choicest
  Of the meat, and laid before him,
Happy in a deed of service,
  Prompted by the love she bore him.
In the hut of Waba-Ogen
  Sat the chief, and gravely listened
To the words her tongue had spoken
  Or from out her eye that glistened.
" Why, my chief, take only hunters
  Your adventurous perils sharing?
They will grow both faint and weary
  From their burdens homeward bearing.
Lead the way with chosen hunters
  And the rest with us shall tarry
As we follow in your pathway;
  Those who can the sick will carry;
Then at night, in sheltered valley,
  Clear the snow, and camp-fires burning,
Shall from upward curling smoke wreathes
  Signal to your Braves returning.
Pause not for a hard day's journey;
  Go where e'er the game shall lead us,
Great or small, or choice or savage,
  Everything will help to feed us.

Be your hunt for Moons continued,
　We shall not be far behind you,
And if you should halt with plenty,
　We shall very quickly find you.
Go where snows are deeper, higher;
　Go where ice is thicker, colder;
Go where Winter is a Warrior,
　Yielding unto warrior bolder!"
After drinking in the music
　Of her words, and gazing, musing,
Flashed at first his eyes in answer,
　All her fire his soul infusing;
Then a cloud of thought came over
　Machikawa's face, that wholly
Changed his mien from light to shadow,
　And he answered, speaking slowly,
"Shall your Chief, though most *your* lover,
　Bid his warriors turn their faces
From the land their fathers' left them,
　And their old men's burial-places?
Shall he leave the cherished wigwam,
　Where, when summer birds are flying,
He his promised bride might welcome?"
　Waba-Ogen, quick replying:

"I will come into your wigwam,
  I will try to aid and cheer you,
If with pride I can sustain you,
  I will be forever near you."
At her feet, in rapture pouring
  Language born of love's emotion,
As his guiding-star he hailed her!
  Worthy all the tribe's devotion!
"But of you I am unworthy
  Till I do the work assigned me;
Till I find the better country
  I must leave my love behind me.
Foremost of my band of hunters
  Be my place, and you, remaining
With the tribe, by noble courage,
  Every fainting heart sustaining."
In the council sat the Warriors
  And the Hunters of the Nation,
Passed the pipe in silence, waiting
  Machikawa's explanation.
Rising 'mid the mute assemblage,
  He the maiden's words repeated,
Adding to them his approval
  Of the project, then was seated.

First the old and then the younger
　　Briefly signified approval.
So few murmurs, Machikawa
　　Named the morrow for removal;
Chose his hunters for the vanguard;
　　Named the chiefs of each division;
For the bearing of the aged
　　And the sick then made provision.
Oh, the days of weary marching!
　　Oh, the nights of cold and hunger!
When it seemed as if the journey
　　Could not be continued longer!
Still, each day, some toiling hunter
　　Found the people, always bearing
Food, and telling wondrous stories
　　Of their leader's skill and daring.
After two moons Machikawa
　　And his Hunters had, by driving
Game into the valleys, gathered
　　Food to wait the tribe's arriving;
But the land for future living,
　　Where henceforth, his people dwelling,
Might in winter find abundance
　　For the pangs of hunger quelling;

Such a country yet he found not,
  So, his force of Braves dividing,
Some he left the game in charge of,
  Some returned the tribe for guiding;
Taking but three trusted comrades,
  Further still the snows exploring,
Forth he started, every danger,
  Every thought of fear ignoring!
After seven Suns had glinted
  Back the rays of setting glory,
All were on the snow reclining
  List'ning to a hunter's story,
And the grateful rest was welcome,
  Hard-fought day their vigor crippling.
List! a Warrior interrupted!
  From a spring the water rippling!
Soon they found the sparkling water,
  From its earthy prison gushing!
Scarce a dancing sunbeam kissing,
  E're beneath the snow-crust rushing!
Spread before them was a glistening
  Plane of purest, dazzling whiteness;
Not a shrub or tree threw shadow
  On the Lake's unclouded brightness.

2

First the snowy shroud removing,
  Then the stone-axe nimbly swinging,
Burst the water's icy fetters,
  Which from out the deep came springing,
And the torch-light, penetrating
  Where the ice mask had been broken,
Lured the fish, as if for learning
  What the brightness might betoken;
Then the Indians, with their flint spears,
  And their tackle, caught such numbers
That their shouts of final triumph,
  Echoing, 'woke the forest slumbers!
Near the spring they made a wigwam,
  Then, on well-baked fish they feasted
To repletion, thinking, each one,
  Sweeter food had never tasted!
In the morning, Machikawa,
  Glancing 'round in admiration,
Said to Spring, and Lake, and Forest,
  Here henceforth shall dwell a Nation!
Here shall end our weary journey,
  Waba-Ogen, I have found it!
Found the place where hunger is not!
  And my tribe shall rest around it.

When the winter snows are deepest,
    And the forest game shall fail us,
This good Lake will still befriend us,
    Hunger's pangs shall ne'er assail us.
By the spring of living waters
    Set they boughs bent to the center,
Bound them well to form the wigwam
    Which the White Rose soon should enter.
Then upon their trail returning,
    With a load of fish they started;
Light of heart and strong of purpose;
    But their Chief was lightest hearted!
For the task by her suggested,
    And by him pursued undaunted,
Was accomplished; here his people
    Would not be by famine haunted.
Toil a pleasure seemed unto them,
    Day by day the task diminished,
'Till at length, the smoke ascending,
    Told their journey nearly finished:
Sunk in slumber, were the people,
    When the Chief and Warriors found them;
But their shouts of welcome, quickly
    Woke to life the woods around them!

When he told them of the country
   And the Lake, the great fish-giver,
Hopeful words and cheerful greetings
   Spoke of dangers gone forever.
On the morn, their march resuming,
   Every face was smiling brighter,
Every step was more elastic,
   Every burden borne was lighter,
Aided by their stoutest Warriors,
   And their Chief, of all the strongest,
Each day's journey seemed the shortest,
   Though it might have been the longest,
Till at length, with shouts of pleasure,
   Lake, and Spring, and Woods, they greeted,
And at night the camp-fire glowed on
   Waba-Ogen's lodge completed.
Though the tribe were proud and happy,
   Yet they were not quite contented
Till the union of their chieftain
   And the White Rose was cemented.
When the sun shone on the lovely
   Bride, as if in warm caressing,
Machikawa proudly claimed her
   As of all, his richest blessing.

All the day was bright and happy,
  Each, with gratitude o'erflowing,
Gave some token, did some service,
  Both their pride and pleasure showing.
Machikawa and his " White Rose "
  Grew the theme of many a story,
In his valor, and her beauty,
  All the tribe were wont to glory.
Strong the people grew, and stronger,
  Prosperous, and close cemented,
By the ties of common country,
  Where no discords were fermented;
And the Lake, in bounteous measure,
  Gave unto these favored ones a
Feast of fish, whenever sought for,
  And they called the Lake, Kegonsa!

WABESA.

N the shore, where the ripples and pebbles at play,
Sang a lay of the lake to an evening in May,
While out on the water, the ripples, for sport,
As they danced along shoreward, helped to distort
The fair mirrored picture the woods tried to throw
From their towering heights on the waters below.
The landscape was lovely as ever the sun,
In the splendor of evening, threw glory upon;
For the queen of the spring had ascended her throne,
And winter on ice-feathered pinions had flown,
And forest and meadow to hail their new queen
Gaily had donned her bright vesture of green.
Every tree wore the richest verdure of spring
When their leaves are the brightest, the glad offering
Of nature released from the death of the mask
Of winter, and life in the sun-shine may bask.

On the carpet of grass, a few rods from the strand,
Where the prospects of water and forest were grand,
Where the trees, though they screened from the sun's
    hottest rays,
Were open, and gave the blue sky to the gaze.

'Mong the tints of the woods, conspicuously white,
The tents of the hunters attracted the sight,
Obtrusive, yet nestling, as willing to hide
Their winter-white walls on the green hill-side;
Whilst scattered in every accessible place
Were the arms and the spoils of the hunt and the chase.

The curtains of eve' were drawn over the sun;
The hunters had washed, and their day's work was done;
The fatigue of their sport made all ready to rest,
And camp-stools and chairs were brought into request;
They talked of successes, made light of their woes,
'Round the fire, whence the smoke-column gracefully rose.
They had waited e'er eating their evening meal
The return of a comrade ,whose ardor and zeal
In the sport he had followed still kept him away
When the rest had returned quite tired of the day;
But waiting is tedious when nostrils inhale
The smell of roast duck, and partridge and quail;
And one who could bear it no longer thus spoke
To his comrades the sportsmen: "This is no joke ;
I propose that we eat; and I'll bet ten to one
We shall see Jim loom up, e'er we've fairly begun."

But the platters were emptied, the coffee-cups drained,
And the long looked for hunter still absent remained;
While surmises and guesses of what could have chanced
Their late tarrying comrade by all were advanced.
Conjecture seemed lost for some new form to take,
When a flash and report far away on the lake

Told them all without word, that their comrade was still
Attracted by something his game-bag to fill.
Speculation on what could have tempted their friend
To linger so long was brought sharp to an end.
Their thoughts from the absent were turned in surprise
To an unlooked for guest who attracted all eyes.

From the gloom of the woods like a king of the night,
An Indian emerged, and advanced to the light
Of their fire, and with gesture of one nobly bred,
Saluted the circle; then raising his head,
" May hunter intrude upon hunters to-night? "
" You do not intrude; as a guest you've a right
To such as our camp can afford; take a seat,
And we'll see about getting you something to eat;
For your language proclaims that you've lived for awhile
Where blanket and moccasin were not the style."
" Oh, yes, I have passed through your schools," he replied,
" With scholars and doctors for honors have vied;
But my scholarly fame to the whirlwinds has flown,
And over my shoulders the blanket I've thrown."
Quoth the hunter, " Who cares where your parchments have
gone,
We greet you as nature's free, unfettered son.
We have all eaten supper but one, who for sport
Appears to have found the daylight too short;
This moment the flash and report of his gun
Came from far on the lake; he must be for fun
Shooting the stars or the mist, one would think,
For out on the waters it looks black as ink."

"I will wait till he comes," said the chief, "if you please,
Or light him a signal on shore, for the trees
Throw a shadow so dense, so heavy, and black,
As well may bewilder him when he comes back."
Taking brand from the camp-fire, the signal soon burned,
Then quietly back to his seat he returned.

"You had better sit up and eat something," said one,
"For Jim is bewitched by some scent he is on;
He may not return for an hour or more."
"His canoe," said the chief, "has just grated the shore."
All sprang to their feet, glad to welcome their friend,
And glad their suspense, too, had come to an end.
Disappointed and weary, the new comer stood
Looking into the fire, in a deep, sullen mood;
He acknowledged their guest without speaking a word,
And he answered no questions; as if he'd not heard
The scores of inquiries that tongue after tongue
In his unheeding ear all the changes had rung.
"Give me something to eat first, for boys, I'll be shot
If such cursed bad luck ever fell to my lot;
I'm as tired as a dog that has hunted all day,
And until I have fed, not a word will I say!"
"Well, fall to and eat; eat your fill; we can wait;
And you too, friend, eat with him, dispatch plate for plate!"

Supper was at length over, cigars passed around,
And his pipe of the red stone the Indian had found;
All smoked on in silence, until Jim broke the spell,
And in slow, thoughtful words 'gan his story to tell.

" Boys, I never before, since first I drew sight
On a bird, have been fooled as I have been to-night!
About sun-down, I was in the river, you know,
Mid-way in the wide-spread, or a little below;
I was pulling for camp with a hearty good will;
So hungry I scarce could my stomach keep still,
When a sound, half a song, half a sigh, made me scan
All about me more closely, and there sat a swan!
A lovely white swan, and most temptingly near,
Undisturbed by my presence, unconscious of fear.
My gun was in range e'er my oar-blades could sink,
And I gave her both barrels before I could think!
She ruffled her plumes, stretched her neck, turned around,
And was gone e'er the echoes in distance were drowned.
The thought that with both of the barrels I'd missed
Was absurd, and no effort I made to resist
The temptation to turn from my course, 'round to where
I had shot, in search for a few feathers there.
But no, I looked everywhere 'round, there were none!
And I turned to come home: there again was the swan!
I have followed that swan down and up the whole stream,
All over the lake, too, the vision I've seen.
Whenever I turned in despair from a spot
She would show herself temptingly near for a shot;
Just now, on the dark lake, about a mile west,
I gave her my last charge, but it, like the rest,
Was wasted, she shook the shot from her like rain,
With a flutter more telling of pleasure than pain.
Then I pulled with a will to get out of her sight,
But she followed me on, till at last, by the light

Of the fire you so kindly had lit, I could see
Her graceful white neck, as if bowing to me.
Even now, if you'll come to the shore, I dare bet
You a hundred, you'll see the swan floating there yet."
"'Twould be useless," the Indian exclaimed, " for this swan
Is the swan of the lake! and 'tis said that the one
To whom she in spring-time the first shall appear
May count on a happy and prosperous year."
" Well," said Jim, " I have seen her, and now that I've made
Her acquaintance, I'd gladly know more of the shade."
" Come, an Indian legend," they called with delight,
" Friend, we beg of you, tell us the story to-night! "
His assent to their wish, with a bend of the head,
He gracefully gave, and then straightway was led
To a tent where the light of the lanterns shone clear
On the circle of hunters assembled to hear.

The Indian commenced: " The tradition I give,
I give in the hope that it longer may live
Than my tribe, which is passing away from the land
Where my fathers were chiefs," with a wave of his hand.
" The legend was told, and its origin takes,
From the first pale-face known in the land of the lakes! "
Then his eye, as if backward, a lurid gleam cast,
And thus he related a strain of the past:

ON THE WAR-PATH.

When Nibwaka and the remnant
 Of his Braves were met returning
To their village, anxious faces
 Seemed to dread their story learning;
For their war-path had been stormy,
 And for every scalp they carried,
As the trophy of a victor,
 They had left a brave unburied!
Still Nibwaka and his stubborn,
 War-worn band, had held together,
Fighting like death-threatened sea-men,
 Fight the most tempestuous weather!
Patakawa, and a band of
 Guards, were left in charge of plunder
And of captives, ta'en by Matchi,
 On a raid, exciting wonder
For its dash, and for its boldness,
 Making captives, leaving gory
Victims, where was thought no danger
 Of the red-man's ruthless foray.

But the weak and weary captives,
　　Faint of heart, and some death-stricken,
Checked their homeward march, and nothing
　　Could their fainting footsteps quicken.
So their chief, relentless Matchi,
　　Took — no danger apprehending —
Nearly all his force, with eager
　　Footsteps, towards their village wending.

'Mong the captives was a maid of
　　Wond'rous beauty, finely moulded;
Such a one as in the arms of
　　Careful love should e'er be folded!
Torn from home, and friends, and kindred,
　　Hopeless now; of life despairing;
Fearing bitterer death than dying,
　　To her death her captors daring!
And her taunts of Patakawa,—
　　Eyes and gestures so assorted,
Though he knew not what her words were,—
　　Almost won the death she courted:
When, from forth the forest arches,
　　Like an opening pack of harriers,
With their war-whoop for a signal,
　　Sprang Nibwaka and his warriors!

Very small resistance met they,
   And the fight was quickly over,
Those who fell not at the onset
   Plunged into the forest's cover;
Patakawa, when he heard the
   Whoop, was startled! fingers playing
With his knife; for he was brooding
   On the scornful maiden slaying;
But the young brave Wawinaki,
   From the ambush, where he waited
For the signal for the onset,
   Saw them; and to rescue fated,
Drew to head his truest arrow;
   And, with yet the war-cry ringing,
Buried it in Patakawa,
   To the dust the savage bringing!
Then, aloud he called, " Wabegon,*
   Hither come to me for shelter,
I will save you, I will guard you,
   Leave him in his blood to welter."
Answering but his tone and gesture,
   Straight she ran to him, and thrusting
Forth her hands, as for protection,
   All her mien betokened trusting;

---

* A flower.

Eagerly he ran to meet her,
    Then in safety, bade her tarry,
While he hurried for the scalp-lock
    It would be his pride to carry!

Why should one so lately dreading
    Indian capture, Indian dealing,
From an Indian, to an Indian,
    Fly with such a change of feeling?
Only this, the soul has language,
    Language other than the spoken;
Soul with soul can hold communion,
    Though the silence is unbroken!

But Nibwaka knew that surely
    Those who had escaped his onset
Would the tidings bear to Matchi
    Ere they saw another sunset.
So he laid his plans for marching
    Quickly, on his path retreating,
Taking counsel with his warriors
    Every accident for meeting.
Wawinaki brought a pony,
    And by sign, and gesture bidden,
By the maiden, found the saddle
    Which ere capture she had ridden.

This, the compact was between them,
  Though no word was comprehended,
His, a love to adoration!
  Hers, that she had been defended.

When the runners told to Matchi
  All the tale of his disaster
He became possessed with fury
  That he could not, would not, master;
Struck to earth the hapless runner
  Who the tidings first imparted,
Swore the boom of flying night-hawk
  Had dismayed the chicken-hearted!
Called him liar! called him coward!
  Thus for fleeing; swore another's
Tongue had spoken for a warrior,
  Thus to slander all his brothers!
But the tidings soon by others
  Fully were corroborated;
Matchi then, with dark eye blazing,
  And with fury unabated,
Turned, and with the yell of demon,
  Sent his startling war-cry ringing!
From the oldest to the youngest
  Warrior, brave, and hunter bringing.
    3

Brief harangue he poured upon them,
  Fierce and harsh, unlike a human's;
Bidding all, in arms and war-paint,
  Straight to answer to his summons!
Then the race began in earnest,
  Fast pursuing, fast retreating,
But Nibwaka, spoil incumbered,
  Thought but of his foe defeating;
Planned to meet him at advantage,
  Speed and power to match with cunning,
Kept his braves in cheerful temper,
  Talked of fighting more than running!

On an evening, as ascending
  To a high and strong position,
They received to added vigil
  Prompt and startling admonition!
As Nibwaka gazed in silence
  On the ruddy sun-set's glowing,
Wawinaki stood before him,
  Silently a scalp-lock showing!
Flashed Nibwaka's eye like meteor,
  As he viewed the bleeding token!
Grasped at once the whole position,
  Though no word had yet been spoken;

Quick the thoughtful, silent chieftain
   Grew the very soul of action,
And the prompt response of warriors
   Won his smiles of satisfaction;
Scanned the strength of his position,
   Words of cheer to each imparted,
Every chance of vantage guarded,
   Then to meet the foe he started!
Matchi's chase had been conducted
   In such wild and hurried fashion,
Told his wrath, his mind had clouded,
   Leaving him the slave of passion;
When he found his foremost warrior
   Arrow pierced, and scalpless, lying,
Nothing could restrain his fury
   From at once the onset trying;
Rang his war-whoop through the arches
   Of the forest — evening tinted —
Sprang his warriors to the combat,—
   From their blades the purple glinted —
Up the hill as they came rushing,
   Sure the fight would soon be over,
Such a shower of arrows greet them,
   Those unstricken sprung to cover.

But the cover does not save them,
  For the ground was well selected,
And each lurking Indian shows a
  Spot by those above detected;
Thus, the reckless charge of Matchi,
  So disastrously ending,
Taught him caution, all the iron
  Of his temper harshly bending!
But the foes were now together,
  One attacking, one defending,
Giving to the fight, the features
  Of a conflict never ending!
Many times the force of Matchi
  Dashed upon the foes they hated;
Every time, by skill and cunning,
  Had their efforts been frustrated!

Nibwaka, having gained possession
  Of a natural fort, concluded
He would turn the tide of action
  'Gainst the foe he had eluded!
Left his young Braves in position,
  Strength'ning each of nature's barriers,
While upon the flanks of Matchi
  Lurked he with his older Warriors.

Matchi, never fearing danger
  From an enemy behind him,
'Left a trail so broad and open
  That a boy at night might find him.
When he reached the rugged fastness
  His advance was sternly greeted
With a welcome prompt, and fatal
  As to foe is seldom meted.
But they rallied from the startling
  Shock that checked their onward rushing,
And with yet determined courage
  For the summit kept on pushing!
When Nibwaka and his comrades,
  Falling on their rear with fury,
Sent a shower of flying weapons,
  That on fatal missions hurry!
Matchi, as the tide of battle
  Turned, to meet it bravely hurried,
In mid course, a whirling hatchet,
  Fairly in his brain was buried!
When the followers of Matchi
  Saw their chief fall, arms extended,
Every hope of conquest vanished,
  That one blow the conflict ended!

Then Nibwaka and his band of
   War scarred heroes, slowly wandered
Towards the peaceful, smiling country
   That the lovely lake meandered.

Wawinaki and Wabegon!
   For the name that he had given
Was adopted by the Indians;
   From a fragile flower deriven.
All throughout the weary journey,
   Every stroke, his arm had warded;
Both from friend and foe obtrusive
   She had carefully been guarded!
Every other one avoiding,
   Fearing; to him ever clinging
Day by day, 'mid blood and havoc,
   And the war-cry ever ringing.
Though heroic fire, love prompted,
   In his soul was nobly burning,
Toward the spot by her made sacred,
   Watchful eye was ever turning!
When the din of conflict slumbered,
   Tomahawk and knife were resting,
When they paused, their strength to gather,
   For the struggle newly testing,

Then he came, by love instructed,
  And, in mien of supplication,
Smoothed the roughness of her pathway,
  Winning smile of approbation;
Thus they journeyed, he adoring,
  She, for safety, to him clinging,
While the thoughts of home, and kindred,
  From her soul were ever winging;
Till, where silvery rippling waters
  Kiss the flower-bespangled verdure,
And while laughing at, reflecting
  All the beauties of their girdure,
They encamped by fair Wabesa,
  And the peaceful hunt renewing,
Strove to heal the wounds, that lately
  Wrought so nearly their undoing.

Wawinaki and Wabegon
  Slowly grew to conversation,
Word by word was comprehended
  With a quick appreciation.
Yet the lovely flower, Wabegon,
  To their foreign soil transplanted,
Drooped and pined, from ever thinking
  Of the scenes by memory haunted!

·When the dangers hourly threatened,
  When the air was rife with danger,
She had little chance for thinking
  Of the time when she, a stranger,
Should be forced to live repining!
  With herself alone communing;
Every memory and emotion
  To the loved and lost attuning!
Wawinaki watched her drooping,
  Saw her trembling; heard her sighing;
And a dread his soul came over
  Lest Wabegon should be dying!
And by love alone incited,
  Knowing not the gulf dividing,
Offered heart, and arm, and wigwam;
  Tremblingly his fate abiding.
Then, she fell to blindly weeping;
  To his nobleness appealing;
Told the cause of her repining,
  Of the anguish she was feeling!
Told him that, as grateful sister,
  She his kindness e'er would cherish;
But e'er she would share his wigwam,
  By her own knife she would perish!

When Nibwaka heard the answer
  To the chief the Flower had given,
All restraint, and all forbearance,
  From his scornful heart was driven;
"Take her then by force," he answered,
  "Why such coward hesitating?
She might well be proud and happy,
  With so brave a chieftain mating."
"Never!" answered Wawinaki,
  "I can love her, I can lose her,
But while I can drive an arrow
  No one living shall abuse her."
Scornfully then laughed Nibwaka,
  "We will see," and forward springing
Toward a hillock, near the water,
  Where the Flower was sadly singing,
Singing sadly to the water;
  For the shades of evening, sinking
Into darkness, of the lost ones,
  Set the maiden sadly thinking!
E'er the chieftain reached the maiden,
  Stood the young man interposing!
Though unarmed, yet lithe and active,
  Quickly with Nibwaka closing!

"Wabegon!" cried Wawinaki,
  "Fly for life across the water!
Fly Wabegon by the birch-bark!
  He will kill the pale-face daughter!"
And Wabegon turned, and saw them
  Fiercely wrestling, catching, tripping;
Seized the paddle, pushed the boat off,
  Into it then lightly skipping,
Plied the paddle, with the strength that
  Danger gives where strength is wanting;
Far into the lake she paddled,
  Then she paused, exhausted, panting!
Hanging from Nibwaka's girdle
  Was his war-club, strong, but pliant,
When he saw that Wawinaki
  Stood before him so defiant,
Wisdom yielded sway to passion,
  And his war-club madly swinging,
Killed the unarmed Wawinaki;
  Then, the weapon from him flinging,
In another birch-bark leaping,
  Plied the paddle swiftly, deeply,
Hoping to make double slaughter
  Of the pair, and thus completely

Banish from his sight the beauty
  That he now sincerely hated
As the cause of doing murder
  He could ne'er have contemplated.
While they paddled from the western
  Sky, up leapt a cloud of sable!
With a wind, by which deep rooted
  Forest trees were proved unstable.
Lashed the lake to boiling billows!
  Drove the spray in crystal showers!
Tore the air with shrieks, like voices,
  At whose 'hest the stoutest cowers!
Out into the foaming caldron
  Both the boats were swiftly driven,
Where it seemed that superhuman
  Strength unto the maid was given;
For her boat, like dancing feather,
  Ever on the crest was carried,
Every threat'ning billow passed her,
  As by skillful fencer parried;
But Nibwaka vainly struggled
  To regain the shore, where, lying
As he left him, was his victim,
  Potently for vengance crying!

In the dark gulf of the waters
  He was swallowed by the frowning
Waves that chased each other madly,
  E'en his cry of anguish drowning.

When the moon rose, and the tempest
  Had subsided, quick as risen,
And the powers of havoc had been
  Once again returned to prison,
Then the Indians on the water
  Searched in everything that floated
For the love of Wawinaki,
  For the maid on which he doted.
Out upon the lake there seemed to
  Flutter garments, purer, whiter,
Than the pure rays of the moon-light,
  Pure as they, but clearer, brighter!
And as all eyes watched the fluttering
  Garments, they could see the maiden
Standing lightly, forming picture
  Of a shallop, fairy laden,
Strained then willing hands at paddles,
  Eagerly, to catch the glancing
Beauty of the fairy figure,
  Lightly as a feather dancing!

But in vain they strained their paddles,
 For the fairy form, retreating,
Into mid-lake led the Indians,
 Then, as if the rescue greeting,
Gracefully a welcome waved them;
 On they came, each paddle straining,
But with awe they pause and wonder;
 For all that was now remaining
Of the vision of the maiden,
 And the robe of fleecy lightness,
Was a swan, at leisure floating,
 Spreading wings of purest whiteness.
And for long at close of even'
 Could the Indians see the vision
Of the maiden, but on nearing
 It, as if in pure derision,
Was but found a swan, disporting
 On the waters, free as ever,
Oft' its snow white wings extending,
 But the Flower returned never!

MONONA.

EARD ye e'er the Indian legend
    Of the young Brave, Anonawa?
Sometimes called Ussowan (Arrow),
    And at others Machekawa.*
He who left the Four Lake garden,
    Left it in its beauty peerless;
Only hunter's weapons taking,
    But at heart of danger fearless.
He had hunted to the Eastward,
    Where the dense woods live in gloaming;
There he met an Indian stranger,
    Far from tribe and nation roaming.
One who in the heat of passion
    His opponent dead had smitten;
And the blood-avenging spirit
    'Gainst his life the doom had written.

*Strong.

So he fled from home and people;
  Life alone but thought of saving;
Safe from that unsparing vengeance,
  Every other peril braving.
Mute the meeting of these Indians;
  Each one knew the other stranger
To his tongue and to his people;
  Yet they neither thought of danger.
For the eye of both looked kindly,
  Fearlessly, though full of question;
Each as asking of the other
  Which should make a first suggestion.
Anonawa made advances
  By an open hand extending,
And the stranger sprang to answer,
  From his eye the welcome sending.
Hunting many days together,
  Faith and friendship yet grew stronger;
As they learned a common language
  Interchange of thought grew longer.
Till at length the Indian stranger
  Told his friend of the disaster
That had made him flee from vengeance,
  Following ever fast and faster.

Told him of the wondrous prairies
    Stretching far as eye could measure;
Told him of the mighty mountains
    And their yellow golden treasure.
" Thou shouldst see the ' Prairie Lily,'
    Lovelier than the fairest flower
That doth deck the earth in summer;
    Richer than the sunset hour.
Could'st thou win the bright Monona,
    Make her meet thy glance with pleasure,
Thou might'st then return in triumph
    With thy bride a warrior's treasure!"

Anonawa left his wigwam;
    Traversed forests, swam the rivers;
E'en the " Father of the Waters,"
    Rushing sea, the land that severs.
Many, many moons he traveled,
    Nothing fearing, naught to grieve him;
Ever hoping, only anxious
    That his hopes might not deceive him.
He had left the woods behind him;
    And the prairie undulating
Greeted him like swelling ocean,
    All his being dominating.

4

But at length 'neath spreading branches
  Of the willows near a river
From the mid-day sun he sheltered,
  Thinking on the future ever.
When there burst upon his vision
  Maiden beautiful as Heaven;
To his gaze enraptured, seeming
  Goddess unto Indian given.
And he murmured, almost fearing
  He might put to flight the vision,
"Surely thou must be Monona!"
  Anxiously, but with decision.
Then his captive ear drank music
  Such as ne'er had silence broken,
When she said, "I am Monona;
  Who art thou my name hast spoken?"
Then he told her of his journey;
  Told her he had come to hover
Near the lodges of her people;
  Told her he had come to love her.
Told her of the four-lake garden,
  Of the lakes in beauty glassing
Summer skies, or like clear mirrors —
  Tints of fleecy cloudlets passing.

Urged that towards the glorious sun-rise,
  She with him would backward travel,
Promising the forest mazes
  Of her path he would unravel.
Long she listened, reading clearly
  In his eye a depth of feeling,
True and tender for her welfare,
  Love, unknown before, revealing.
Then she answered Anonawa:
  "Thou so many suns hast striven,
That Monona of the prairie
  To thy wigwam should be given,
I will go with thee, young Hunter,
  Leave my people, *all* behind me;
When the West is red at sunset,
  For the path thou'lt ready find me.
I will bring our fleetest horses,
  Lest e'er we have crossed the prairie
They o'ertake us; then thy scalp-lock
  Some Ute chief would proudly carry."

Anonawa with Monona
  By his side, like spirit creatures,
Pressed their horses all the night long,
  Racing with the flashing meteors.

In the morning, 'neath the shelter
　　Thick that fringed the water-courses,
Rest they sought, rest and refreshment,
　　For themselves and for their horses.
As the young man gazed in rapture,
　　Breathing words by love suggested,
Pensively Monona listened,
　　Long his strain was unmolested.
Thus she answered, "Anonawa!
　　I have seen thee in my dreaming,
Seen thee scan the broad lake's surface
　　When the morning sun was beaming.
Seen thee standing on the headland,
　　Life and joy in every feature,
While the fanciful lake mirror,
　　Giant-like enlarged thy stature.
Seen thee watch until the monarch
　　Of the clouds came slowly sailing,
Then thine arrow sped like lightning,
　　Guided by an eye unquailing.
Struck to death the noble eagle,
　　From his sailing downward swooping,
Plunging in the clear lake's bosom,
　　Wings outspread but talons drooping."

Thus responded Anonawa:
  " Thank the Love that led me to thee,
And awoke within my bosom
  Longing to behold and woo thee.
We will marry, not as Indians,
  But as the white father teaches,—
He who journeyed from the sun-rise,
  And about the white Christ preaches."

On a gentle Sabbath morning,
  When the sun in beauty smiling
Kissed the lake — the lovely wonder,
  Every glance to her beguiling,
In the water stood Monona,
  By her side, the pale-face father;
He had promised to baptize her
  And her brave young chief together.
And he asked the Indian maiden,
  As she stood — by far surpassing
Every beauteous thing in nature
  That the crystal lake was glassing,
This he asked her: " When I sprinkle
  Water on thy head and bless thee,
By what name as new-born daughter
  Of our faith, shall I address thee?"

And the lovely maiden answered:
  "Father I will bear alone a
Name by which my mother called me;
  I will always be Monona.
But if names must needs be mingled,
  Father, listen to thy daughter,
Take not thou Monona from me,
  But give it unto the water."
And from all the tribe assembled,
  Far across the lake was thrown a
Joyous shout of glad approval,
  Hailing the fair lake — Monona.

MENDOTA.

DO you know the mossy headland,
　　With its em'rald-hued corona,
Throwing shadows deep into the
　　Bosom of the lake Monona?
Just behind it lies the garden,
　　Wond'rous in its wild-wood glory!
Need we marvel that the Red Man
　　Told its fame in many a story?
For its beauty has few rivals,
　　Either 'mid the gems of nature,
Or where art on nature's landscape
　　Deftly touches every feature.
'Tis no wonder they forsook it
　　With reluctance, ever casting
Backward glances, speaking sorrow
　　Deeply stamped and everlasting.
Faint around us grow the traces
　　Of the Indian, like the dying
Autumn daylight, or the rushing
　　Night sound of the wild birds flying.

Still the summers bring some scion
 Of the forest, singly straying,
Silently, amid the shadows
 Both of woods and race decaying!
Ah, those native forest children
 Recked not of the hidden story
Of a race that ere their coming
 Was already old and hoary!
Not to them had e'er been whispered
 From the green mounds, undulating
O'er their garden, aught of people
 Their traditions all pre-dating.

Seated in the wild plum orchard,
 Where the Spring-time air was scented
By the perfume from the blossoms,
 Wafted with a wealth unstinted,
Three young Indian boys were talking
 Of their father's skill and daring;
Each one rivaling another,
 When their sire's renown comparing:
One was named "The Loon," the "Screamer."
 Nameless yet remained another,
Save "The son of the Canoe Man."
 Young Mendota was the other.

One was boasting of the scalp-locks
   That his father's hand had taken;
Telling of him in the war-dance;
   How his whoop the woods had shaken.
" He had crossed the mighty river;
   With the warlike Sioux had striven; .
'Round the painted post, when dancing,
   Deepest had his axe been driven."
Another boasted of his father
   As most skillful on the water:
" Like an arrow fled the birch-bark,
   When her flight his paddle taught her.
Who but he, the dancing shallop,
   Through the white-caps could send flying
Faster than retreating foemen,
   Who for life the stroke were plying ?
Were it not that 'Arm that sweepeth'
   Made the boat fly like the swallow,
Some, whose scalps your father mastered,
   Still would chase and war-path follow!
See, Mendota still is working.
   Still a flint-tipped arrow making,
Chipping, scraping, feather-gumming,
   As for some great undertaking.

We of hick'ry make our arrows —
  Make them strong and heavy headed;
But Mendota, would-be hunter,
  Using shaft by panther dreaded."
Sprang Mendota from the earth mound,
  Like a young Adonis standing,
Looking down upon his comrades,
  Audience and respect commanding:
" All your blunt and harmless arrows
  Scarce the deer would scare from feeding;
If with this I fairly strike him,
  I can track him by the bleeding.
And *you* boast your father's honors!
  Scalp-locks won by stealth in fighting;
Stealing, cat-like, on unguarded
  Foeman, not a cover slighting.
When a conquered chief lay dreading
  Of his scalp bereft to perish!
Then *my* father scorned to rob him
  Of the prize that warriors cherish!
Those around him stood and questioned,
  Why for fame so little caring?
' On the happy hunt,' he answered,
  ' Let him go, his honors wearing!'

True, your father sweeps the paddle,
  Best and strongest of the nation;
Victor crowned in every contest,
  Cause for all your exultation;
But *my* father wears the bear claws —
  Claws of savage bear, that yielded
Life and trophies to the death-stroke,
  From the tomahawk he wielded!
And the panther's skin I carry
  Tells of hunter scorning danger,
Armed with club and knife, he reft it
  From the peerless forest ranger!
Down he threw the bloody trophy,
  Smiling as successful hunter,
Naught of pain — though sorely wounded —
  Talked, but of the fierce encounter.
All our braves are on the war-path:
  Some will come, and some lie sleeping
'Neath the green and crimson carpet,
  Crimsoned, by their death wounds weeping!
After nearly two moons' labor,
  See, my arrow is completed;
I will leave you with the women,
  Or around the camp-fire seated;

I will go into the forest,
    On the hunter's trail remaining
Till I change my arrow's color,
    Losing it, or game obtaining."
Straight he turned his back upon them,
    Heeding neither laugh nor jeering,
With his bow and single arrow
    In the forest disappearing.
High the boy's heart beat within him,
    With the consciousness of going
On his first assay of manhood;
    Full of youthful ardor glowing!
Nothing but his robe of panther,
    O'er his shoulder thrown, he carried,
Serving both for couch and raiment,
    In the forest while he tarried —
Save the moccasin of buckskin,
    Neatly fashioned, quill'd and beaded,
And a knife by thong suspended —
    All equipment that he needed;
Through the forest slowly wending,
    Grace in every limb and feature!
Beauty, to its beauty adding,
    Nature's child alone with nature!

Thus he wandered, thoughtful, musing,
  Of the morrow ever thinking,
Till he reached the rocky headland
  As the sun was grandly sinking,
Throwing o'er the Lake Mendota
  Such a flood of golden grandeur
That both eye and tongue were spell-bound
  By the exquisite expandure!
Sun and sky and lake commingle
  Color in such rich profusion
That the heart seeks voice, entreating
  Fitting words for its effusion!
Massive color, bold in outline,
  Fading into blended glory,
Telling to enraptured gazers
  Beauty's most bewitching story!
And Mendota gazed in wonder,
  All his soul the scene entrancing;
Like the chiseled statue, standing
  Motionless, an arm advancing;
Thus he stood, until the rival
  Pink and pearl and purple, blending,
Softened into light-blue ether,
  Solemnly the sunset ending;

Then he turned, as one awaking
  From a dream, reluctant, sighing,
Loth to leave the living picture
  Every sunny clime outvying!
Ate of what the lake and forest
  Freely gave to those acquainted,
Spread his panther-skin and entered
  Sleep's blank realm, by dreams unpainted.

Ere the east had caught the tinting
  Of the first gray dawn of morning
Up he sprang, refreshed, from slumber;
  Donned the panther's rude adorning;
No more careless was his bearing,
  But, while listening acutely,
Restless flashed his eyes like meteors,
  Traveling swiftly, softly, mutely;
Not a chirp of bird, or murmur
  Of the woods, but well was noted;
To the chase, the youthful hunter,
  Every energy devoted!
Thus he sped, until he halted
  By the winding broad Yahara!—
In the east the sun, arising,
  Threw aloft his red tiara —

Stealing, cat-like, through the bushes,
　To the water's edge advancing,
Keenly listening for the breaking
　Of the forest silence,— glancing
Quickly at each sign of nature.
　Ah! why do the branches quiver
Just beyond the hillock rising
　At the sharp bend of the river?
Scarce the air can hear his movements,
　Though his steps are nearly flying,
Till the gentle breath of morning,
　From the spot, toward him, is sighing;
Then, while creeping nimbly forward,
　Nature's stillness yet unbroken!
Not a taint, or sound of warning,
　Of his presence giving token,
Till, within an easy bow-shot,
　He perceives, in quiet, feeding,
Three good deer, unconscious, careless,
　His approach unknown, unheeding!
One brave stag with branching antlers
　Shook his crest, and bid defiance
To the forest! he, the monarch,
　Seemed to stand in self reliance!

And the boy's heart madly bounded;
　　But his nerves were all unshaken,
As to head he drew the arrow!
　　Having each precaution taken —
Twice, he tried, if sure and steady,
　　He could aim behind the shoulder,
But the intervening brush-wood
　　Made him choose a method bolder;
Rose erect, like silent shadow,
　　Every nerve his pressure tightening,
And before the stag had seen him,
　　Sped the fatal shaft like lightning!
Then, by instinct, he embodied
　　The antique, the great Apollo!
Form of beauty, standing rigid;
　　Sight and soul the arrow follow!
Right arm gracefully withdrawing,
　　Still his left, the bow extending;
On the flying arrow's fortune
　　Every faculty is bending!
But a moment stands the statue
　　Breathless, most intently watching,
E'er the boy's heart leaped to manhood,
　　All the hunter's ardor catching!

One brave bound the stag attempted,
  Then stood still, except the shivering
Of the death-stroke, for the arrow,
  Deep sunk in his flesh, was quivering!
E'er the stag had time to rally,
  Recklessly the hunter darted
On him, and with knife deep driven,
  Life's sustaining current parted!
Then he stood, intently watching,
  Where the gasping and the sighing
Of the fallen forest monarch
  Told the noble stag was dying!
And his heart was touched to sadness
  By the piteous glance, appealing!
For an eye of matchless beauty,
  More than instinct, seemed revealing.
But the hunter's labors claimed him;
  He the deer must skin and quarter,
And upon the saplings hang it —
  Young trees, mirrored by the water.
Thus he toiled until the mid-day
  Sun shone on his labor finished,
And upon a boy's exultant
  Satisfaction undiminished;

  5

With one ling'ring glance of pleasure
　　At the quarry, all unheeding
Food or rest, with earnest purpose
　　On the home trail he was speeding.
Quietly, into the village
　　Walked Mendota, quite suppressing
Every look of triumph, waiting
　　Comrade's questioning and guessing;
First, " The Screaming Loon " assailed him —
　　Son of him the scalp-locks wearing —
Gave to him a mocking welcome,
　　Mimicking his stoic bearing;
Called aloud unto the women,
　　" Ho you there, the deer are plenty
In the forest, you may hunt them,
　　For Mendota's hands are empty!"
Silent stood the youthful hunter,
　　Scarce a lip's contemptuous curling;
But the pliant panther mantle
　　Round his form in triumph furling,
Till the son of " Arm that Sweepeth "
　　Said, " Where has my brother tarried?
Bloody is the flint-tipped arrow
　　He into the forest carried!"

Like the sun, on sudden bursting
    Through the clouds the earth oppressing,
Lit Mendota's eye in triumph;
    And the thought his mind possessing —
Though it compensated taunting —
    Burst its bonds, and but addressing
Him who had the arrow noted —
    While unseemly boast suppressing —
Told him all about his hunting,
    Where he slept, and then related
All the details of his triumph,
    With the victor's joy elated.
" Oh my brother, had you seen him
    As the morning's breath he greeted,
Nobler stag than e'er a hunter
    With a single shaft defeated!
You with me will take the birch-bark,
    We can paddle like our fathers;
It is light, and dry, and dancing,
    And the roughest sea it weathers;
I have left my prize in safety;
    'In the saplings I have swung it
Out of danger; 'mong the branches
    Bending o'er the water, hung it."

Lightly glanced the birchen vessel
  O'er Monona, from the agile
Paddling of the eager rowers
  Swiftly, flew a bark so fragile;
Soon Monona lay behind them,
  And Yahara then ascending
'Gainst the current, far more slowly
  Traced the boat the river's wending;
Till at length the bending willows
  Meeting midway, as if hiding
Where Mendota found an outlet,
  Yielded to the birch-bark's gliding.
And the broad lake spread before them,
  Rich again in sun-set glory!
Speaking to admiring senses,
  Grand, but silent, oratory!
Both, by impulse, paused and floated,
  Gazing on the grand combining
Of the mass of living colors
  Blended o'er the sun's declining!
Not a breath the water ruffled,
  Almost mirror-like it slumbered;
When the boys resumed their paddles,
  'Twas with strokes more slowly numbered;

Thus, partaking of the spirit
 Of the glorious, quiet even',
Scarce their boat disturbed the water,
 From the light impetus given.
Still they paused not, but yet floating
 With a stroke so light and wary,
Undisturbed, they passed the wild duck,
 On the lake's great tributary.
Silence on the river rested,
 Not a breath the air disturbing,
For the night had spread her mantle,
 All the evening tints absorbing!
Still they held their course unerring,
 'Till, the wooded hillock reaching,
They prepared to rest till morning,
 Carefully their light boat beaching;
Then, these children of the forest,
 Nature taught, in all resources,
Made repast and sank to slumber;
 Like the child the mother nurses!

Morn had scarcely in the Orient
 Shown the night its russet banner,
'Ere the boys arose from slumber,
 And in gleeful, boyish manner,

Laughed, and called unto the day-break:
  " That the sun, his chariot's eager
Coursers, might urge on more quickly!
  For the light was yet too meager;"
Ah! the grey is growing brighter,
  As the night rolls up her sable;
To discern the quarry, hanging
  Safely, soon the boys were able!
"See you, where the branching antlers
  Yonder white-oak limbs are bending?
Branch of tree and antlers branching,
  Look, the morning grey is blending!"
Mute in wonder stood his comrade!
  All the story he had told them
Was surpassed; 'twere worth the journey,
  Thus suspended to behold them!
Hard they labored, till the light boat
  With the precious freight was loaded;
Into mid-stream then they darted,
  Like a steed whose flanks are goaded.
Scarce the sun had left the tree tops,
  When Monona lay before them;
On the prow they placed the antlers,
  Honoring the bark that bore them!

Soon with steady, measured effort,
  Midway in the lake they floated,
Asking, by their eager glances,
  If they must return unnoted?
Quick, the son of " Arm that Sweepeth "
  Said, " Mendota, hist! look yonder!
Those are not the women only,
  Down the wooded banks who wander? "
Quite erect the boy had risen,
  'Gainst the wale on paddle leaning,
Eagle-like, his vision reaching
  O'er the water intervening!
Then he answered, " Brother hunter,
  Neither squaws nor papoose meet us;
Home returned are all our warriors,
  And they line the shore to greet us! "
'Ere again his paddle dipping,
  One shrill whoop, the lake resounded!
Like the swallow, o'er the water,
  Then the airy shallop bounded!

Short the space, till 'neath the garden,
  They have landed with their treasure;
Mute are all the dusky warriors,
  But their eyes the antlers measure!

For no hunter of the nation
   Such a conquest ever boasted!
Such a pair of branching antlers
   Over lodge had ne'er been posted!
Almost irksome was their silence
   To the youth, who hoped for praises
And approval of his efforts;
   But his deed the tribe amazes!
Till his father, noted, lying
   In the boat, the blood-stained arrow!
And from out his sheath he drew one,
   Tipped with flint head, sharp and narrow!
In the boat, beside the other,
   Quietly he stepped and laid it,
Saying, "Boy, when next you need it,
   Here's a second one to aid it!"
Quick as thought the impulse seized them;
   Many braves their best selected,
Into the canoe they tossed them,
   Till there lay a store collected
Of such arrows that their owner
   Might a chieftain's envy kindle!
Some were strong and heavy pointed,
   Others, slender as a windle

He whose totem was an oak tree
    By the lightning rudely riven!
Called the boy to stand before him,
    Pointed to the arrows given,
Then — as chief of all the Nation
    Turned around, his arm extending,
Claiming audience of his warriors,—
    Royal tone and gesture blending,—
Told them " Though returning victors
    From the war-path, all the chaunting
Of their deeds would be outnumbered
    By the song of this boy's hunting."

High above them in the garden,
    Shrill the women's voices sounded;
When he heard his mother call him
    Nimbly up the bank he bounded;
Here, it was no longer needful
    That the stoic, quiet bearing
Of the Indian should restrain him,—
    Nothing for appearance caring —
Straight he ran to meet his mother;
    She, her arms about him twining,
Lavished on him fond endearments,
    In those tones of tender whining,

Sounding sweetly by her uttered —
    Breathing love and pride commingled;
Sometimes, like the notes of tinkling
    Bells of silver, lightly jingled.
Listening kindly — softly laughing —
    To the pleasant, rippling murmur;
In his eye the light of loving
    Glowed with ardent warmth of summer!
Answering gently her caresses,
    Answering thus, her benison,
" When our braves are gone, my mother,
    I can bring you venison."

And the boy in time was chieftain,
    Bravely for his tribe contending,
'Till the tide of tireless workmen —
    Ever open hand extending —
Swept the country, and the hunter
    Spent the day the deer in tracking,
But to see it wrested from him
    At the deadly rifle's cracking!
Then the hatchet they unburied;
    Long and far the war-path treading;
For the white man's friendship fighting,
    Brother's blood for stranger shedding!

But at length the winged arrow
  With the death the fates had written
For Mendota, found his bosom,
  And to earth the chief was smitten!
" Bear me homeward," said Mendota;
  " To the lake of sun-sets bear me;
In my boat upon the water
  For the happy hunt prepare me."
Home they bore the wounded chieftain;
  Not a listening ear could note a
Sound, as in his boat he drifted,
  On the bosom of Mendota!
In the ev'ning, when the western
  Sky gleamed like a searing cauter,
The CHIEF upon the LAKE Mendota
  Gave his spirit to the water.

www.ingramcontent.com/pod-product-compliance
Lightning Source LLC
Chambersburg PA
CBHW030021030726
47499CB00008B/3072